TEACHING SUGGESTIONS

In addition to providing an enjoyable listening experience for young children, this book provides a unique opportunity to build auditory perception of initial consonant sounds. Children should be encouraged to listen carefully to each command to determine what is the same about the words in the commands. After the discovery that several of the words in each command begin with the same sound, learning can be extended (according to the individual's readiness) by having a child (1) give alternate commands using the same consonant sound; (2) name other words that begin with the same sound; or (3) find pictures in magazines of items that begin with each sound.

If appropriate to the maturity level, you may wish to identify the letter associated with a given sound.

The Authors

The Kingdom
of Kibalakaboo

by Carl F. Brown
and
Marion R. Hodes

Illustrations by Kathleen McCarthy

THE INSTRUCTO CORPORATION • PAOLI, PENNSYLVANIA

This book is dedicated to
the many children and teachers
who never had fun with phonics.

The Authors

The Instructo® Corporation   •   Paoli, Pennsylvania

Long, long ago, in the middle of a small, magical sea, there was a small, magical island called the Kingdom of Kibalakaboo.

Have you ever heard of kumquat trees, kurrajong, or quebracho trees? Have you ever seen an albatross, a kookaburra, or a dodo bird? Do you know a wombat, a wallaby, or a yak? You could find these strange trees and birds and animals in the Kingdom of Kibalakaboo.

In a beautiful palace in the middle of a beautiful garden lived King Kibala and his wife, Queen Kaboo, and their son, Prince Baboo.

One thing troubled good King Kibala. He knew his people were happy. He saw them smile. But never, ever, never had he heard them really laugh.

"We must find a way to make our people laugh," said King Kibala to the queen. "We will go to other islands and find out what makes people really laugh."

The next morning King Kibala called all of the people and birds and animals of the kingdom together. "Queen Kaboo and I are going on a trip. While we are gone Prince Baboo will be your king."

And the king and the queen left.

Prince Baboo sat alone in the shade of the kurrajong tree and wondered and wondered and thought and thought. What does a king do? "I know," he said. "My father gives orders and commands. That's what I will do."

The prince called everyone together and gave his first command, **"I command . . . I command . . .**

the baboons to feed berries to the bears!"

And did the baboons feed berries to the bears?

Of course, the camels wore caps and capes.

"I command . . .

the donkey to teach the dodo bird to dive!"

And did the donkey teach the dodo bird to dive?

Of course, the donkey taught the dodo bird to dive.

By this time almost everyone in the kingdom was laughing. Who had ever seen anything so ridiculous as camels wearing caps and capes? And what could be funnier than a donkey trying to teach a dodo bird to dive?

And so the young prince gave more commands.

"I command the farmers to feed feathers to the fish."

And did the farmers feed feathers to the fish?

Of course, the farmers fed feathers to the fish.

"I command the goat to play a guitar for the geese."
And did the goat play a guitar for the geese?

Of course, the goat played a guitar for the geese.

"I command the horses to put the hippos into the house."
And did the horses put the hippos into the house?
Of course, the horses put the hippos into the house.

"I command the jugglers to jump over the jack-o-lanterns."

And did the jugglers jump over the jack-o-lanterns?
Of course, the jugglers jumped over the jack-o-lanterns.

"I command the kittens to put keys on the kookaburras."

And did the kittens put keys on the kookaburras?

Of course, the kittens put keys on the kookaburras.

"I command the lizards to lead the lobsters to the lake."

And did the lizards lead the lobsters to the lake?

Of course, the lizards led the lobsters to the lake.

"I command the monkeys to make a motor out of magnets."

And did the monkeys make a motor out of magnets?
Of course, the monkeys made a motor out of magnets.

"I command the nobles to rub noses with their neighbors."

And did the nobles rub noses with their neighbors?
Of course, the nobles rubbed noses with their neighbors.

"I command the penguins to push the peacocks into a puddle."

And did the penguins push the peacocks into a puddle?

Of course, the penguins pushed the peacocks into a puddle.

"I command the quail to sew quarters on a quilt."

And did the quail sew quarters on a quilt?
Of course, the quail sewed quarters on a quilt.

"I command a reindeer to put a ring on a rooster."

And did the reindeer put a ring on a rooster?
Of course, the reindeer put a ring on a rooster.

"I command . . .

a sailor to put a saddle on a sea horse."

And did a sailor put a saddle on a sea horse?
Of course, a sailor put a saddle on a sea horse.

"I command a turtle to sing a tune to the tiger."

And did a turtle sing a tune to the tiger?
Of course, the turtle sang a tune to the tiger.

"I command the visitors to play violins for the vegetables."

And did the visitors play violins for the vegetables?
Of course, the visitors played violins for the vegetables.

"I command the wallabies to give waffles to the worms."

And did the wallabies give waffles to the worms?
Of course, the wallabies gave waffles to the worms.

"I command the youngsters to play yoyos with the yak."

And did the youngsters play yoyos with the yak?
Of course, the youngsters played yoyos with the yak.

"I command the zebras to zigzag in the zoo."

And did the zebras zigzag in the zoo?
Of course, the zebras zigzagged in the zoo.

Just then the king and queen returned to the Kingdom of
Kibalakaboo. They heard roars of laughter. They hurried to
the palace to find out what was happening. When they came to
the garden imagine their surprise when they saw . . .

Baboons feeding berries to the bears,

Camels wearing caps and capes,

Donkeys teaching dodo birds to dive,

Farmers feeding feathers to the fish,

Goats playing guitars for the geese,

Horses putting hippos into the house,

Jugglers jumping over jack-o-lanterns,

Kittens putting keys on kookaburras,

Lizards leading lobsters to the lake,

Monkeys making motors out of magnets,

Nobles rubbing noses with their neighbors,

Penguins pushing peacocks into puddles,

Quail sewing quarters on a quilt,

Reindeer putting rings on the roosters,

Sailors putting saddles on the sea horses,

Turtles singing tunes to the tigers,

Visitors playing violins for vegetables,

Wallabies giving waffles to the worms,

Youngsters playing yoyos with the yak,

Zebras zigzagging in the zoo.

The king and queen could hardly believe what they saw. The queen started laughing, and then the king started laughing. Everybody on the island laughed at the funny things young Prince Baboo made the people and animals do.

If you could be king of the small, magical Kingdom of Kibalakaboo, what commands would you give?